Sarah Lolley

Emily and the Mighty Om

Illustrations by
Sleepless Kao

SIMPLY READ BOOKS

In the summer, someone new moved in next door to Emily.

His hair was white and his face was wrinkled, but his eyes always seemed to sparkle. His name was Albert.

Every afternoon, Albert twisted his body into all kinds of strange positions on his front lawn.

"It's called 'yoga,'" he told Emily, who watched from her front porch.

When he finished, Albert sat with his legs crossed and chanted a single word: "om."

"What's 'om'?" Emily asked.

Albert smiled dreamily. "It's a magic word that everything understands—people and animals, trees... even rocks. It helps me feel quiet and relaxed."

Emily thought this was a little strange, but she was also curious to see if it really worked.

She whispered "om" to the plants in the living room...

...and her collection of rocks...

...and her cat.

But they didn't seem any different.

Emily noticed that every afternoon, Albert was in a different yoga pose. "Asanas," he called them.
    Some of the poses looked easy, but others looked really difficult.

One day, Emily came home to find Albert all twisted up.

"Are you okay?" Emily asked.

Before Albert could answer, a lifeguard cycling past leaped off his bike and ran over. "Dude! You're totally stuck!"

"Can we help?" Emily asked.

Emily and the lifeguard leaned in to hear what Albert had to say.

"O...," he managed in a muffled voice. "O...!"

"You heard him!" the lifeguard shouted. "He wants a PHONE. When I get stuck, I call my mom. He wants to call for help, too."

Emily was pretty sure she knew what Albert
had really said. But the lifeguard was an adult.
Well, almost. She decided not to say anything.

The lifeguard pulled a cell phone from his
pocket.

But Albert simply shook his head. "O...!"
Albert said again, sounding stressed.

Two police officers driving by saw the commotion and pulled over to help.
"O... O...!" they heard Albert say.

"I've got it!" one of the officers declared.
"Whenever I get stuck, I go into my garden to
relax. He needs a garden GNOME to make him
feel in touch with nature."

Emily was very sure that's not what Albert
was trying to say. But she knew better than to
argue with the police.

The police officers zoomed off and returned with a gnome from the garden at the library— and with the librarian, who insisted on coming to make sure her gnome stayed safe.

The officer placed the gnome between
Albert's arms. But Albert didn't budge.
  "That's highly suspect," she commented.
  "O...! O...!" Albert insisted.

"A POEM!" the librarian shouted. "That must be what he wants. A relaxing POEM!"

Emily was certain the librarian was wrong. But would anyone listen to her?

The librarian took a pen and paper
from her purse and quickly
wrote a poem called
"Ode to Albert."

> *Oh Albert! What horrendous luck!*
> *You seem to be profoundly stuck!*
> *We tried a phone, we tried a gnome*
> *But clearly what you need's a poem!*
> *So here it is. It's short but true*
> *And hopefully of help to you.*

But it didn't work.

   "Didn't you like the poem?" the librarian
asked, sounding hurt.

   "O...!" Albert pleaded.

"O...! O...!"

The grown-ups all began to talk at once.

"He needs a COMB!" the lifeguard announced.

"No—we need to build a DOME!" the police officers argued.

"Maybe he needs to go to ROME!" the librarian countered.
 "Or should we just leave him ALONE?" one police officer
asked the other.

Ignoring everyone, Emily sat down cross-legged
beside Albert.
  She closed her eyes and took a deep breath.

"Ommmmm,"

she chanted quietly.

"Oh," everyone exclaimed. "Ommmmmm!"
   The grown-ups sat down on the lawn with
Emily and tried to cross their legs as she had.
They took deep breaths and all chanted "om."

Everything became very quiet. The wind died down and the clouds stopped speeding across the sky. The leaves on the trees stopped rustling. Everything relaxed.

After the third "om," there was a soft popping sound as Albert's legs and arms came unstuck.

"Whew!" Albert said, standing up shakily. "That sure was a difficult pose. Halfway through I got nervous that I wouldn't be able to do it, and because I was nervous, I got stuck."

He turned to Emily. "Thank you," he said, pressing his hands together and bowing his head.

"Namaste."

It wasn't the last time Albert got stuck, but from then on, everyone knew what to do.

And they knew what to do whenever they got stuck, too.

To Mikio Masuda—SK

Published in 2014 by Simply Read Books
www.simplyreadbooks.com
Text © 2014 Sarah Lolley Illustrations © 2014 Sleepless Kao

We gratefully acknowledge for their financial support
of our publishing program the Canada Council for
the Arts, the BC Arts Council, and the Government
of Canada through the Canada Book Fund (CBF).

LIBRARY AND ARCHIVES CANADA CATALOGUING IN PUBLICATION

Lolley, Sarah
    Emily and the mighty om / written by Sarah Lolley ; illustrated by
Sleepless Kao.

ISBN 978-1-897476-35-2

    I. Sleepless Kao II. Title.

PS8623.O47E65 2011   jC813'.6   C2010-905668-X

Book design by Elisa Gutiérrez
Interior text set in Museo Sans

Manufactured in Malaysia
10 9 8 7 6 5 4 3 2 1